T0368362

The Last Egyptian Standing

The Last Egyptian Standing:

The Great Egyptian

Part 2

Story and Written by,

Mo Nassah

authorHOUSE®

AuthorHouse™ UK
1663 Liberty Drive
Bloomington, IN 47403 USA
www.authorhouse.co.uk
Phone: UK TFN: 0800 0148641 (Toll Free inside the UK)
*   UK Local: (02) 0369 56322 (+44 20 3695 6322 from outside the UK)*

Published by AuthorHouse 04/10/2025

ISBN: 979-8-8230-9213-5 (sc)
ISBN: 979-8-8230-9214-2 (e)

Library of Congress Control Number: 2025903762

Print information available on the last page.

This book is printed on acid-free paper.

CONTENTS

Contents

INTRODUCTION

An introduction to this would be first a thank you to my Mother that has always helped me any time she can with whatever she can in life, as she gets older as well as I the Author. A thank you to all those in the family, and any friends, that purchased the books that I have written thus far about this true story in my life, and other stories to present date. An introduction to write the entire Novel a Book even on its own, is a magnitude, as I, MN80M continue, so does the title MN80M within the books and not in real life title as some did until now and on until the year 2025 to 2026 once the 2011 Egypt revolution continued story until the 11th February 2011 was/is the main story to be completed and written within three Books and a Novel once possible. The years pass soo quickly, and now MN80M owns the entire country, and not just everything created when this true story commenced in 2011 such greatness for me I know, as Author, yet a tremendous responsibility when owning everything and all. MR and MRS SUPER MYSTERY would agree knowing I own every country and more, and are still talking to me, MN80M, and MR MYSTERY is still the same. The country Egypt has been divided, and the Sinai is now a new country called, The Sinai of Egypt in the year 2024'. MN80M-THE-SPECIAL-ONE-MALE remains as he was in life in 2011 yet moved onto another accommodation, and the first story, yet weaker. The strength of MN80M-THE-SPECIAL-ONE-MALE is depleted mainly from love to others and not to MN80M-THE-SPECIAL-ONE-FEMALE, as much as he would have liked, the life remains in the Egypt revolution only, and not personal after the Revolution, in Egypt. This short book is part 2. Part 3, at the end of the year 2026 will be able to contain much more detail than, has done and is in life to read and know. MN80M-THE-SPECIAL-ONE-MALE owns every country in the World, and that is not a lie. MN80M-THE-SPECIAL-ONE-MALE is getting older, as with the time it takes to write a book, of this nature, something easily nurtured by MN80M-THE-SPECIAL-ONE-MALE.

AUTHOR CHAPTER INTRODUCTION

The Chapters are much less than the first book or possibly more. The Second book is a part of three books on the true story that has yet been released public since the First one in the year of 2011. The lists of chapters are written on the following page and pages to this Author Chapter Introduction. The titles of the chapters are just as flawless as the written text herein about the true story during the Egypt 2011 Revolution. These parts have yet to be read and are already done in the physical form by MN80M-THE-SPECIAL-ONE-MALE.

CHAPTER TEN

Slingshot

MN80M-THE-SPECIAL-ONE-MALE remains with MN80M-THE-SPECIAL-ONE-FEMALE as he launches back with his slingshot towards the on-coming fire of bullets and bricks and rocks from the broken pavement during this revolution.

MN80M-THE-SPECIAL-ONE-MALE pulls back his MN80M-SLINGSHOT and releases it to fire out towards those on-coming with fire and bullets and bricks and rocks they throw out towards MN80M-THE-SPECIAL-ONE-MALE location. He then runs forward some while reloading his MN80M-SLINGSHOT with more MN80M-MARBLES.

12:03, TAHRIR SQUARE, CAIRO, EGYPT
FEBRUARY 2nd 2011
MN80M-THE-SPECIAL-ONE-MALE IS AMONG

MN80M-THE-SPECIAL-ONE-FEMALE AND HER TEAM

MN80M-THE-SPECIAL-ONE-MALE remains well with his team not so far in their defence of the country and not like the others in their battle for power internal of cities and for some of those out of the country wanting the country for their own desirement. Gun shots are heard and people are scattering to save their own lives as well as scattering for the own lives. The tens of thousands are clear evident by MN80M-THE-SPECIAL-ONE-MALE of their groups in divide. Unlike her, MN80M-THE-SPECIAL-ONE-FEMALE and her team that have surely remained vigilant.

<>>>Flash Forward<>>>
2012, Cairo, Egypt.

The woman in the electric blue hat runs into the hotel lobby with her blonde sister as MN80M sits down to drink a coffee in the five star hotel in the mega-complex City Stars Buildings. The two women are waiting eagerly to talk to MN80M.
Flashback

CHAPTER ELEVEN

Sister

12:03, TAHRIR SQUARE, CAIRO, EGYPT

FEBRUARY 2nd 2011

MN80M-THE-SPECIAL-ONE-MALE IS AMONG

MN80M-THE-SPECIAL-ONE-
FEMALE AND HER TEAM

MN80M-THE-SPECIAL-ONE-MALE looks up with passion into the sky to see if he can notice his eagle flying above all as usual, yet has not seen the eagle since the last time when he got out of the taxi near to the Tahrir Square with MN80M-THE-FIRST-SISTER that he just told to get into a taxi again and go home as he had a feeling the place would erupt as it clearly has done with tens of thousands of people in battle. MN80M-THE-SPECIAL-ONE-MALE thinks for a moment as he looks around at the hundreds of

3

thousand people that are entering and exiting Tahrir Square, many without fear against each other, he remembers an hour before MN80M-THE-SPECIAL-ONE-FEMALE's team got closer to her and him, while he was up near the METAL HUTS.

11:03, TAHRIR SQUARE, CAIRO, EGYPT
FEBRUARY 2nd 2011
MN80M-THE-SPECIAL-ONE-MALE IS ALONE
ON TOP OF THE METAL HUTS AMONG
SEVERAL DOZEN PEOPLE THAT ARE NEAR
AN ENGLISH MAN. HE MOVES IN QUICKLY
IN A DEFENCE AND OUT OF INTEREST
MODE WHILE A DOZEN MEN JUMP OFF
THE METAL HUTS. MN80M TAKES POSITION
OVERLOOKING IT ALL FROM ABOVE AND
NEAR THE ENGLISH GENTLEMAN.

MN80M-THE-SPECIAL-ONE-MALE
"Hello, where are you from? Did
you come from England?"
MN80M says to the English man, as
he then moves in closer to him.

ENGLISH GENTLEMAN
"I came from the Emirates"
MN80M-THE-SPECIAL-ONE-MALE
"That's nice".

MN80M-THE-SPECIAL-ONE-MALE looks at his backpack on his back and the ticket says Iraq on it. The man was lying to MN80M-THE-SPECIAL-ONE-MALE and he knew it.

MN80M-THE-SPECIAL-ONE-MALE
"It's too dangerous to be up here, you should get down."
MN80M-THE-SPECIAL-ONE-MALE said to him
as he then starts to look at the tens of thousands of
people that continue to pour into Tahrir Square,
Cairo, Egypt as the Revolution continues. MN80M-
THE-SPECIAL-ONE-MALE looks down at the
huts from the top down and notices posters being put
up of the MN80M-PRESIDENT of Egypt, then up
left onto a heard of people and camels charging into
the Square with no remorse at those staying in the
crowds in the square, Tahrir Square, Cairo, Egypt.
MN80M-THE-SPECIAL-ONE-MALE
"It's a Hit"

MN80M-THE-SPECIAL-ONE-MALE quickly looks at the gentleman again and at all around and says, "It's a Hit". Meaning those coming in are hired to kill, they are seen charging in on the camels with whips and whipping from over ten feet of height to those walking lower than the Camels height with the men on the camel whipping them all in sight. The Pro-President ones in Egypt against ten thousand anti President ones in the square towards MN80M's right hand side, as he then views the first punch and rocks being thrown and the camel charge from the left into the right centre of Tahrir Square. "It's a Hit" MN80M said. MN80M notices what others do not notice.

CHAPTER TWELVE

Metal Huts

11:17, TAHRIR SQUARE, CAIRO, EGYPT
FEBRUARY 2nd 2011
MN80M IS ON TOP OF THE METAL HUTS
UP AWAY FROM THE ONSLAUGHT COMING
INTO THE SQUARE AGAINST THOSE
REMAINING AND NOT BEING MOVED
AS THE PRESIDENT SAID THEY SHOULD
NOT LINGER AROUND THE SQUARE
TOO LONG. MN80M LOOKS AROUND.

MN80M-THE-SPECIAL-ONE-MALE smiles as he saw some of the men get closer to the Metal Huts, with flags of pictures of the president and whips in their other hand, whipping people, and tens of thousands of people rushing in with them to support them beating up anyone inside of Tahrir Square, to leave. Some of them joined forces just at the moment those did with Molotov Cocktails being thrown and rocks broken from the curb to throw at those remaining. MN80M-THE-SPECIAL-ONE-MALE looks up into the sky, and smiles, his Eagle in flight, his Eagle in sight.

<>>>Flash Forward<>>>
February 11 - 2011 Old Cairo, Egypt.
MN80M is digging, looking for his blood.
Flashback

12:09, TAHRIR SQUARE, CAIRO, EGYPT
FEBRUARY 2nd 2011
MN80M-THE-SPECIAL-ONE-MALE IS AMONG
MN80M-THE-SPECIAL-ONE-
FEMALE AND HER TEAM

MN80M remembered one hour ago when he was up on the Metal Huts. MN80M is glad the English gentleman got off and away, and looks around at MN80M-THE-SPECIAL-ONE-FEMALE, and her team. He wants to save them all, and tell them like he told the English Gentleman to go home and be safe to be safe and get off of there, and be safe, yet he knows they too are here to die if need be for the country their own lives they would give. Pro-Egypt as the MN80M-SISTER-ONE said, MN80M agrees with her on that to be said to all, instead of how they are all going, instead of into destruction and death every day.

CHAPTER THIRTEEN

Personal

12:09, TAHRIR SQUARE, CAIRO, EGYPT
FEBRUARY 2nd 2011
MN80M-THE-SPECIAL-ONE-MALE IS AMONG
MN80M-THE-SPECIAL-ONE-
FEMALE AND HER TEAM

MN80M-THE-SPECIAL-ONE-MALE
"Are you ok?"
MN80M-THE-SPECIAL-ONE-FEMALE
"Yes".

12:10, TAHRIR SQUARE, CAIRO, EGYPT
FEBRUARY 2nd 2011
MN80M-THE-SPECIAL-ONE-MALE IS AMONG
MN80M-THE-SPECIAL-ONE-FEMALE AND
HER TEAM THAT DISPERSE QUICKLY.

MN80M-THE-SPECIAL-ONE-MALE

"Where did they go?"

MN80M said to MN80M-THE-SPECIAL-ONE-FEMALE as he looks around at the square. She looks at her clothing and ring on her clean hand of both of her hands and she smiles. The shattering sounds of glass smashing to pieces on impact is then heard near their feet from a Molotov Cocktail homemade grenade type missile is thrown near them onto the concrete. MN80M-THE-SPECIAL-ONE-FEMALE moves fast from the petrol burning smell on the floor next to her and them all from the onslaught toward them all.

12:12, TAHRIR SQUARE, CAIRO,
EGYPT. DAY: FEBRUARY 2nd, 2011.
THE SUN IS SHINING BRIGHT AMONG
THE TENS OF THOUSANDS OF PEOPLE.
MN80M-THE-SPECIAL-ONE-MALE,
MN80M-THE-SPECIAL-ONE-FEMALE
IS BOTH TOGETHER STANDING IN
TAHRIR SQUARE WITH HER TEAM.

MN80M-THE-SPECIAL-ONE-MALE
Don't let them fail.

MN80M-THE-SPECIAL-ONE-FEMALE
I won't, never.

MN80M-THE-SPECIAL-ONE-MALE
Tell them to come forward to me on the right side.

MN80M-THE-SPECIAL-ONE-FEMALE
Our side.

MN80M-THE-SPECIAL-ONE-FEMALE
runs fast in her MN80M-SPECIAL-WOMEN-
SHOES, towards her team and shouts out, "run
quick. Run towards me quick, my side."

MN80M-THE-SPECIAL-ONE-MALE
I thought you said, "Our side".

CHAPTER FOURTEEN

Her Team

A TEAM OF PEOPLE COME RUNNING
TOWARDS THEM BOTH ON HIS RIGHT SIDE.

TAHRIR SQUARE, CAIRO, EGYPT. DAY:
FEBRUARY 2nd, 2011 TENS OF THOUSANDS
OF PEOPLE CAN BE HEARD.
MN80M-THE-SPECIAL-ONE-MALE, MN80M-
THE-SPECIAL-ONE-FEMALE ARE BOTH
TOGETHER STANDING IN TAHRIR SQUARE.

<>>>Flash Forward<>>>
2015, London, England, United Kingdom.

Reco awaits training with MN80M near to the garages he is
in. MN80M can still read his mind while keeping anything
Telepathy a top secret most highest secret with ecceterestrial
and ecceterainiu the same and not being used much by
he, MN80M-THE-SPECIAL-ONE-MALE, and those he

passed them onto especially the connections by shaking their hands and approval at the same time verbal saying so.
<u>Flashback</u>

A TEAM OF PEOPLE POINT OUT BEHIND
MN80M-THE-SPECIAL-ONE-MALE, MN80M-
THE-SPECIAL-ONE-FEMALE BOTH BACKS
AS THOUSANDS MORE OF THE PEOPLE ARE
RUNNING FAST AND THROWING THINGS
TOWARDS THEM LIKE MOLOTOV COCKTAILS
AND BRICKS FROM THE BUILDINGS DERELICT
NEAR THEM BOTH.
MN80M PREPARES HIS SLINGSHOT
TO STOP THEM ATTACKING.

<>>>Flash Forward<>>>
2021, London, England, United Kingdom
The Queen of England. "Mohammed, you paid off all the debts of every country, you own them all now."
Flashback

TAHRIR SQUARE, CAIRO, EGYPT.
DAY: FEBRUARY 2nd, 2011.
12:20 THE SUN IS SHINING BRIGHT AMONG
THE TENS OF THOUSANDS OF PEOPLE.
MN80M-THE-SPECIAL-ONE-MALE, MN80M-THE-
SPECIAL-ONE-FEMALE ARE BOTH TOGETHER
STANDING in TAHRIR SQUARE. HER TEAM
STAND TO HIM AND HERSIDE NEXT TO THEM
BOTH, AS THEY GATHER TOGETHER TO
DEFEND, EGYPT, TO DEFEND THE COUNTRY.

MN80M-THE-SPECIAL-ONE-MALE
"Thank You!"
"All of you stay on her side."

MN80M said out loud near shouting out the words. "Stay on her side" as he continues to scan the area for any further threats. The Camel Charge has come to an end, and the men riding them with whips have gone on, onto some side streets where certain battles remain blatant in a blood all over the street on some streets from people battles days prior.

CHAPTER FIFTEEN

A Team

12:20, TAHRIR SQUARE, CAIRO, EGYPT
FEBRUARY 2nd 2011
MN80M-THE-SPECIAL-ONE-
FEMALE AND HER TEAM
ARE IN TALKS WITH EACH OTHER
FOR THE FIRST TIME IN THAT DAY
ALL TOGETHER AS SHE LEADS HER TEAM.
MN80M-THE-SPECIAL-ONE-FEMALE

"Do not look at what we have lost,
look at what we have gained."

MN80M-THE-SPECIAL-ONE-FEMALE said to her
team, as the heat of the day continues, and she remembers
MN80M-THE-SPECIAL-ONE-MALE once said so to her
those words. Her team are ready and they are searching for
more trouble makers to stop them, and to stop anything
negative together with MN80M. She looks up into the sky

like him, and then back at them all. There is not much she can do on her own, her ANCIENT CAERULEA RING on her finger lights up, blossoms out some, and then back in on her ring finger on her right hand. Her Team saw this, and knew, so did MN80M from a far. Danger is near. MN80M-THE-SPECIAL-ONE-FEMALE smiles.

> MN80M-THE-SPECIAL-ONE-FEMALE
> "Let's Go!"

MN80M-THE-SPECIAL-ONE-FEMALE starts to move fast in the direction her ring glows more.

<>>>Flash Forward<>>>
2025, London, England, United Kingdom

MN80M is walking near Paddington station on route to Sarah Siddons statue, a man and his adult daughter notices him. MN80M continues walking to his destination not knowing he will be falling in love with her or her twin sister. MN80M walks on nervously.
Flashback

MN80M-THE-SPECIAL-ONE-MALE AND MN80M-THE-SPECIAL-ONE-FEMALE COME TOGETHER HER ANCIENT CAERULEA RING BLOSSOMS OUT BRIGHT INDIGO PURPLE COLOUR SHE SMILES. MN80M MOVES CLOSER TO HER AND DEFLECTS A MOLOTOV COCKTAIL NEAR SMASHING INTO HER HEAD IT FALLS NEXT TO THEM ALL SMASHES AND FIRE AND GLASS SCATTERS

NEAR THEM ALL FROM THE PETROL INSIDE THE
HOMEMADE GRENADE TYPE OF MISSILE.

"No one run" shouts out MN80M in English then Arabic.

12:22, CAIRO, EGYPT. DAY: FEBRUARY 2nd, 2011.
MN80M-FIRST-SISTER HOME
THE SUN IS SHINING BRIGHT OUTSIDE AND
HER FOUR DOGS ARE BARKING IN AND OUT
OF THE BALCONY. MN80M-THE-FIRST-SISTER
IS SPEAKING WITH HER DOGS WHILE THE
TELEVISION IS ON THE NEWS CHANNEL LIVE.

MN80M-FIRST-SISTER

"Come and eat your food come and get it" she says to her
dogs, now on route running to her kitchen area for the bowls
on floor their food inside. She looks around and then at the
television to see if she notices anything new, even her brother
possibly on the news, yet nothing new just yet is shown.

12:22, NASR CITY, CAIRO, EGYPT.
DAY: FEBRUARY 2nd, 2011.
MN80M-THE-SPECIAL-ONE-MALE HOME
MN80M's flat is empty in Cairo Egypt.

12:23, CAIRO, EGYPT. DAY: FEBRUARY 2nd, 2011.
MN80M-FIRST-SISTER HOME

MN80M-FIRST-SISTER
"Come and eat your food I said and come
and get it" she says to her dogs.

CHAPTER SIXTEEN

Time Together

<>>>Flash Forward<>>>
2024, London, England, United Kingdom

Reco is trying to get the ecceterestrial back to MN80M and not to the ones that steal and keep stealing them to get power and rule the World.
Flashback

12:22, CAIRO, EGYPT. DAY: FEBRUARY 2nd, 2011.

MN80M-THE-SPECIAL-ONE-MALE   asks
MN80M-THE-SPECIAL-ONE-FEMALE

"What did you tell your team." She responds, "Don't look at what you have lost, look at what you have gained." She said. He says back in a reply out loud, "each other", or "me". MN80M said. "For me" she says. They both smile, "we have each other". "True" I know the saying a meaning Soo beautiful to say. Thank you!" Said MN80M.

The men in her team are in battle with some of those coming in Anti-Country, they are not pro Egypt. MN80M quickly did with his slingshot a marble to one of the men they defeating with knives big enough to be a samurai sword. The marble hits one of them in the face. He stops immediately among two others. They remaining remain in battle. MN80M puts his hand into his pocket then takes out more for the slingshot.

MN80M-SISTER-ONE HOME
2011 CAIRO, EGYPT
THE SISTER WITH HER DOGS REMAINS SAFE
AT HER HOME. SHE'S ON THE
TELEPHONE TO HER MUM.

MN80M-SISTER-ONE
"I Told him he can come today once it's done, it's been like that since January 25th 2011. Most blood on streets a week ago when it all started until now of seven hundred thousand people have been killed, it's very dangerous out there." Said MN80M-SISTER-ONE.

12:57 TAHRIR SQUARE, CAIRO, EGYPT.2011
MN80M-THE-SPECIAL-ONE-MALE SPEAKS
TO MN80M-THE-SPECIAL-ONE-FEMALE
THEN RUSHES OFF TOWARDS THE ROAD
EMPATHY-TARGET-17 WAS AS HE THEN
FIRES BACK SEVERAL OF THE SPECIAL

MN80M MARBLES IN HIS SPECIAL POUCH
TOWARDS TARGETS WITH MACHETTE'S
IN THEIR HAND LIKE AN HOUR PRIOR.

MN80M-THE-SPECIAL-ONE-MALE
"I will come back" "stay strongest" "get your team to safety."

MN80M-THE-SPECIAL-ONE-FEMALE
"I will, we will be over in that road and up to you any time
you need us, we will try to hold them off from coming
in from that side." She said to him as she moves fast now
towards that street and road.

TAHRIR SQUARE, CAIRO, EGYPT. DAY: FEBRUARY
2nd, 2011. 12:47 THE SUN IS SHINING BRIGHT
AMONG THE TENS OF THOUSANDS OF PEOPLE.
MN80M-THE-SPECIAL-ONE-MALE, with MN80M-
THE-SPECIAL-ONE-FEMALE are BOTH TOGETHER
STANDING in TAHRIR SQUARE.

MN80M-THE-SPECIAL-ONE-MALE
Don't let them fail I said.

MN80M-THE-SPECIAL-ONE-FEMALE
I won't, never, I said.

MN80M-THE-SPECIAL-ONE-MALE
Tell them to come forward to me on the right.

MN80M-THE-SPECIAL-ONE-FEMALE
I did. Our side.

MN80M-THE-SPECIAL-ONE-FEMALE runs fast towards her team and shouts out, "run towards me quick, my side."

MN80M-THE-SPECIAL-ONE-MALE
I thought you said, "Our side".

A TEAM OF PEOPLE COME RUNNING TOWARDS THEM BOTH ON HIS RIGHT SIDE
MN80M-THE-SPECIAL-ON E-MALE, and MN80M-THE-SPECIAL-ONE-FEMALE are BOTH TOGETHER STANDING in TAHRIR SQUARE.
A TEAM OF PEOPLE POINT OUT BEHIND MN80M-THE-SPECIAL-ONE-MALE, and MN80M-THE-SPECIAL-ONE-FEMALE BACKS AS THOUSANDS MORE OF THE PEOPLE ARE RUNNING FAST AND THROWING THINGS TOWARDS THEM LIKE MOLOTOV COCKTAILS AND BRICKS FROM THE BUILDINGS DERELICT NEAR THEM BOTH LIKE THE OTHER SIDE.

Flash Forward ------------------_____

2025 - LONDON, ENGLAND, UNITED KINGDOM. 21:30 - NIGHT MN80M is ALONE IN A HOSPITAL COMMANDING AN ARMY AND RUSSIAN MILITARY AS MARSHALL LAW. MN80M IS IN SPECIAL CONTACT WITH PEOPLE VIA SN1 OR SN2 SENDING OUT POSTING A MANUEL AS A NEW CONTRACT WITH RULES AND TRAINING METHODS FOR AN ELITE TEAM OF WOMEN TO

BE A FORCE. MN80M IS TYPING ON HIS PHONE
BEFORE SENDING OUT TO THEM.

- Able to kill for me.
- Working for me only, the owner of every country.
- Have intent to shoot to kill anything anytime for me,
MN80M the Owner.
- Be strong-minded with a will to success to then succeed.
- Able to work good on your own.
- Able to tell me anything at any time and everything.
- Able to shoot to kill and have no remorse.
- New Rules can be created anytime by me, MN80M.
- Have zero tolerance to crime at me the Owner.

Sniper Training ; introduction
The 7th of each month is training for 17 Turkish Russian
females young women in the Russian military or Russian
army. 1 female of japanese origin, Japan.

Only you 18 plus one Ukrainian female is permitted to learn
this and use it. Teaching is not allowed of what I teach.

- Plus Sandra, you all know her name, can teach if I tell
her to something for flying the Aeroplane, she being then
19 of you learning in training, plus one female Ukrainian,
assisting teaching, and one learning = 21.
Manuel:

SNIPER TRAINING MANUEL: 2025.

Sniper Rifle Training: elite force team only.

Step 1;
How the bullet goes into the sniper rifle. (Learn how many bullets a sniper rifle can sustain and how many to go into it total)

Step 2;
How the shoulder support works and why? (Between right shoulder and top neck chest area)

How to aim. (See the target O° in the middle down center then step 4)

Step 4;
How to pull the trigger/Leaver for the bullet to come out onto the target. (Target in sight. Aim center, hold breath in deep breath, then aim focus the same then pull trigger/leaver shot)

Step 5;
The scope. How to look through the scope step 3, to 5. (Keep looking through the scope at target area or person)

Step 6;
Pulling the trigger/leaver on target. How to shoot. (Now you learned, hold breath and fire sniper gun bullet to target perfection)

Step 7;
Double shots. How to handle double shots. Straight shot straight shots. No hesitation. No waiting. Always double shots to any target even if dead on first shot.™ (Aim fire) Manuel;

More to training will be added here. End of Training Manuel.

MN80M STOPS TYPING AND POSTS IT OUT TO THEM AT SEA ON AN INTELLIGENCE SHIP THE WOMEN ARE ON.

Flashback_____

TAHRIR SQUARE, CAIRO, EGYPT. DAY: FEBRUARY 2nd, 2011. 12:52 THE SUN IS SHINING BRIGHT AMONG THE TENS OF THOUSANDS OF PEOPLE IN TAHRIR , CAIRO, EGYPT

MN80M-THE-SPECIAL-ONE-MALE, MN80M-THE-SPECIAL-ONE-FEMALE are BOTH TOGETHER STANDING in TAHRIR SQUARE, MN80M-THE-SPECIAL-ONE-MALE TAKES OUT HIS SLING SHOT AND MARBLE POUCH AND FIRES BACK LAUNCHING MARBLES AT THEIR ROCKS BEING THROWN BREAKING EACH BRICK AND ROCK THEY THROW.

TAHRIR SQUARE, CAIRO, EGYPT. DAY: FEBRUARY 2nd, 2011. 12:53 THE SUN IS SHINING BRIGHT AMONG THE TENS OF THOUSANDS OF PEOPLE. MN80M-THE-SPECIAL-ONE-MALE, MN80M-THE-SPECIAL-ONE-FEMALE are BOTH TOGETHER STANDING in TAHRIR SQUARE WITH THEIR TEAM NEAR.

CHAPTER ONE ZERO ONE: 7.
MN80M-THE-SPECIAL-ONE-MALE approached the side road running faster than ever, then comes to a halt. He turns around first, then with his fist, his right hand to floor, like a near punch, he silently then says, "Freeze Time". He looks up at everyone. First he noticed one of the marbles from his sling shot in the air towards the people in revolt, and looks up at MN80M-THE-SPECIAL-ONE-FEMALE standing in a frozen position like everyone else except for him, MN80M-THE-SPECIAL-ONE-MALE. He looks around some. "Unfreeze", he said. Everything was back to normal again in Tahrir Square, the battles and skirmiches continue to come through near the metal huts and from the bridge with the lions on them easily. MN80M-THE-SPECIAL-ONE-MALE takes out his marble pouch and loads more into his slingshot.

TAHRIR SQUARE, CAIRO, EGYPT. DAY: FEBRUARY 2nd, 2011. 12:03 THE SUN IS SHINING BRIGHT AMONG THE TENS OF THOUSANDS OF PEOPLE. MN80M-THE-SPECIAL-ONE-MALE, MN80M-THE-SPECIAL-ONE-FEMALE are BOTH TOGETHER

STANDING in TAHRIR SQUARE. "Are you ok!?!." He said, "yes" she responded.

Flash Forward………..…
London England United Kingdom 2025
MN80M-THE-SPECIAL-ONE-MALE is in contact to three angles of People, with the Egyptian Revolution over a decade and nearly a half ago. In the past now. He sits commanding new recruits during Marshall Law that he is, Marshall Law.

Flashback……………………………
2011, TAHRIR SQUARE, CAIRO, EGYPT.
MN80M is in Tahrir Square looking at everyone around him wondering how this day will turn out and become. MN80M-THE-SPECIAL-ONE-FEMALE Is next to him.

MN80M-THE-SPECIAL-ONE-FEMALE
"I'm here."

CHAPTER SEVENTEEN

Empathy Targets

12:59 TAHRIR SQUARE, CAIRO, EGYPT.2011

MN80M Stands on his own, and wonders for a few seconds, the way the war or battle is going on as he looks slowly from left to right. He knows now what to do. And starts making his way towards the Metal Huts, to where he saw the first punch being thrown from one man on the right hand side in the centre of the magnitude of a crowd, as the men on the camel charge continue on in. He starts to move fast now. He notices a group of men, with a machete and moves in alone fast to them before they chop down onto a male with white skin. MN80M quickly moves in onto them, "He is with me", he said as the Egyptian Male holding the machete nearly killed the white male, and then to quickly get the male out of that area near the tanks next to the museum. They both move away, "Where are you from?" asks MN80M, "I am from America." Said the male. "I live just around the corner from here, where do you live?" he then asked and answered again to MN80M's response of, "Nasr City, Cairo, Egypt is where I live, yet I am from London, England to the response from the white male, "Quick they are blocking up the road that I live on, we might be able to get through with me because I live there, you can come if you like to get off the streets and away from here." The Target had said to MN80M-THE-SPECIAL-ONE-MALE. "Ok" MN80M said as he looks around with people close to his sight with blood all over them and the battles ferocious continues around him and near him. MN80M walks off with him, as they both move fast, and he looks back at the men bleeding, blood on the street, the road, the curbs smashed to pieces with dozens of rocks left on the floor as weapons for people to use once battles commence and continue and more people coming and going into the Tahrir Square and ones with machete and Molotov Cocktail's that are being used upon the people defending the Tahrir Square as the main battle ground for all Egypt battles at this time. "What is your name" said MN80M. 'nai' he said to MN80M whom knew it backwards, and that he might be one of the Targets. "And what is your name" he said as they both continued to walk towards his rented accommodation through the battles and skirmishes there in Tahrir Square. "Mohammed is my name" said MN80M, and he kept walking with him until he got into his apartment/flat. He located his target, the MN80M-Empathy-TARGET17. As he could be one of those reporting fake news on the TV the television or throwing fuel to the fire and getting weapons for some of them to use during the revolution. They both keep walking until getting into his flat off of one of the roads next to Tahrir Square.

<u><>>>Flash Forward<>>></u>
2024, London, England, United Kingdom MN80M apartment/Flat.

MN80M is getting back the ecceterestrials from those that are stealing memory, ghemmory and foam and all the ecceterestrials with different names that are owned by him, including live and greater and lucky and truth.

<u>Flashback</u>
<u><>>>Flash Forward<>>></u>
2021, Cairo, Egypt MN80M's HOME.
Some more people are stealing with the same usual gang. MN80M Stops them yet they continue to come back.
<u>Flashback</u>

MN80M-EMPATHY-TARGET17 APARTMENT/FLAT.
CAIRO, EGYPT 2011 FEBRUARY 2nd.

The empathy target is rushing around in his flat looking for his laptop and other electric device, then speaks out, "I'm just looking for my laptop I might be able to report this all on the news. You should do a blog." He said. "Is it ok to film from the bedroom window some." Yes sure it is go ahead.", So MN80M-THE-SPECIAL-ONE-MALE Starts recording some machete battles on the street down below with them barricading the road. He could hear nai the MN80M-EMPATHY-TARGET17 lying over the telephone in the APARTMENT/FLAT. CAIRO, EGYPT 2011 as if to his mum, but it was to his dad that was CIA. MN80M knew he was a target. MN80M hears him tell him he might be able to get on CNN live news. As MN80M continues filming, the street battle from the bedroom window. MN80M looks out of the window to the street below and notices the men fighting one man with a machete in his right hand lifting it up and then near down onto the shoulder of another man like what happened to nai. Yet this time MN80M was unable to help as he did raise his arm and block the other one from doing that to nai prior to coming up to his flat. MN80M records with his small camera what is occurring, as the battles on the street, remain going on. MN80M notices the man has blood all over him, his clothing and arms, hands. MN80M continues filming from the window at nai's home, property he rents. Then goes into his living room, from the bedroom and then noticing MN80M-EMPATHY-TARGET17 has all his equipment out ready on the table in his APARTMENT/FLAT. CAIRO, EGYPT 2011. The phone rings, nai remains very professional, and within seconds is live broadcasting on CNN with his picture on the screen and voice from the telephone answering questions live about the revolution. Both MN80M and MN80M-EMPATHY-TARGET17 are in shock in his APARTMENT/ FLAT. CAIRO, EGYPT 2011, nai, is live on air, the only one, and he is not exaggerating, he is telling the truth, reporting the truth. MN80M stays for a while then makes a decision to leave to locate MN80M-THE-SPECIAL-ONE-FEMALE. "I think I can go now. Good luck with all you are doing." MN80M said to him, knowing he is not one to think about and stop, as he is speaking the truth, unlike all the other reporters that millions of Egyptians were hunting down because they were reporting lies, and exaggerating the truth during over eight hundred thousand of Egyptians were killed the past week to that day on the second of February 2011. "Ok then dude! Hope you get out and home safely." MN80M-EMPATHY-TARGET17 said to MN80M-THE-SPECIAL-ONE-MALE. Then he walked down with him to see his buildings main doors the people had barricaded in case any onslaught came into them all living there. They moved a few things and then MN80M-THE-SPECIAL-ONE-MALE walks out of the door.

13:35 TAHRIR SQUARE, CAIRO, EGYPT
FEBRUARY 2011
MN80M-THE-SPECIAL-ONE-
MALE IS ON HIS OWN,
DOWN TO THE STREETS.

MN80M is making his way through to the Tahrir Square moments away, notices one female on the phone giving a fake report, to an Arabic news channel, saying the Military are killing them all, she is lying, and is now located by MN80M.

MN80M-THE-SPECIAL-ONE-MALE approaches her, and shakes his head, as to not do what you are doing to her the female, now an MN80M-EMPATHY TARGET18. Then he walks on fast, in towards Tahrir Centre and past the barricade that lets him pass with ease, and no questions asked of him. MN80M-THE-SPECIAL-ONE-MALE moves fast in, on route to where he and MN80M-THE-SPECIAL-ONE-FEMALE were before. Her team are not in sight, and towards the right, the two main Egyptian Military Green Tanks are there and not moving, while hundreds into

Mo Nassah

thousands of people surround and continue to come in and out of Tahrir Square in a battle for the Square, and country. MN80M looks at her, then at her CAERULEA RING on her finger on her right hand. MN80M-THE-SPECIAL-ONE-FEMALE clinches her fist some, and then looks up at MN80M.

CHAPTER EIGHTEEN

The Country And Our Lives

13:37 TAHRIR SQUARE, CAIRO, EGYPT
FEBRUARY 2011
MN80M-THE-SPECIAL-ONE-FEMALE IS AWAY
FROM HER TEAM THAT ARE AROUND THE
ARMY TANKS, IN A DEFENCE MODE.

MN80M-THE-SPECIAL-ONE-MALE looks up towards the army tanks and people and then the sky for the eagle. He notices her team in battle then the sound of gun shots with one person next to him near dropping to the ground, on yet no impact of the bullet.

MN80M-THE-SPECIAL-ONE-MALE heard the sound of a machine gun.

He moves faster than normal. MN80M-THE-SPECIAL-ONE-MALE is making his way to the next entry area of the square. MN80M-THE-SPECIAL-ONE-FEMALE

See's him and smiles waving her arms around so he can see. He does so and notices a man coming out of a tent with a machine gun. MN80M-THE-SPECIAL-ONE-MALE gets closer to her and her team with her as she MN80M-THE-SPECIAL-ONE-FEMALE realizes the severity. "We cannot do this on our own, we need the military but they are only watching." Said MN80M-THE-SPECIAL-ONE-FEMALE, "We need more help",

"We need more help." She said again.

MN80M-THE-SPECIAL-ONE-MALE tells her, "Go to your team, and then go home. Today's battles will be tomorrow the same or similar go now while you can and return tomorrow."

MN80M-THE-SPECIAL-ONE-FEMALE smiles, then closes her eyes for a second, looks at her ring, then runs off into the crowd and direction of the army tanks.

MN80M-THE-SPECIAL-ONE-MALE watches her from a far until she vanishes among the tens of thousands of people.

13:52 TAHRIR SQUARE, CAIRO, EGYPT
FEBRUARY 2011
MN80M-THE-SPECIAL-ONE-FEMALE IS AWAY
FROM HER TEAM THAT ARE AROUND THE
ARMY TANKS, IN A DEFENCE MODE AND
CLOSENS TO THEM ALL SIGNALLING TO
THEM ALL TO LEAVE. THEY DO LEAVE.

SHE LOOKS BACK ONE LAST TIME TO MN80M-THE-SPECIAL-ONE-MALE.

<u><>>>Flash Forward<>>></u>
2021, Cairo, Egypt.
"Yes! Global Incentives is paid to every country" "Just as I have told them to do so, The World Bank of the World."
<u>Flashback</u>

<u><>>>Flash Forward<>>></u>
2021, Cairo, Egypt.
MN80M is sitting down at home. "Everything is still the same.".
<u>Flashback</u>

MN80M-THE-SPECIAL-ONE-MALE looks at the time, 13:53, and looks again at his MN80M-SQUARE-SHAPED-WATCH, Then onto his MN80M-Coffee-Bean-HandScan-Device, Brightly shining, then he moves forward to try to see MN80M-THE-SPECIAL-ONE-FEMALE and her team in a battle on the street as they retreat for now to safety, as the weeks past until then. MN80M stops, looks up and says, "I'm Here,' "I'm Here!" Said, MN80M-THE-SPECIAL-ONE-MALE.

CHAPTER NINETEEN

Our Lives

13:52 TAHRIR SQUARE, CAIRO, EGYPT
FEBRUARY 2011

MN80M-THE-SPECIAL-ONE-MALE approaches the side road running faster than ever once again, leaping in the air jumps high then to the ground, then comes to a halt. He turns around first, then with his fist, his right hand and fist to floor, like a punch, he then says, "Freeze Time". He looks up at everyone. First he noticed one of the marbles from his sling shot in the air towards the people in revolt, and looks up at MN80M-THE-SPECIAL-ONE-FEMALE standing in a frozen position like everyone else except for him, MN80M-THE-SPECIAL-ONE-MALE. then looks around some. "Unfreeze", he said. Everything was back to normal again in Tahrir Square, the battles and skirmiches continue to come through near the metal huts and from the bridge with the lions on them easily. MN80M-THE-SPECIAL-ONE-MALE takes out his marble pouch and loads more into his slingshot. "I'm here!"

CHAPTER TWENTY

"Our Lives Continue!"

2011 - TAHRIR SQUARE, CAIRO, EGYPT.

MN80M-THE-SPECIAL-ONE-MALE is, standing in Tahrir alone. MN80M-THE- SPECIAL-ONE-FEMALE is not far with her team safety surrounding her from any onslaught. NIGHT.

Flashback_____

FlashForward_____

2025 - MN80M is in LONDON, ENGLAND, UNITED KINGDOM

OWN ROOM IN A HOUSE. Looks at his device, the screen, the door bell ringing, a house next to the old ceiling to floor windows on Church Street, in another house not far, in his own room. Awaiting Housing by the Government.

2025. Still leading as Marshal Law, with new teams being trained. Couching words, guidance and direction MN80M teaches them, the young Women in the Army or Military, how to be a Sniper, and Fly Jets. His Wording on the World Wide Web:

Words and Numbers on the Screen, on an MN80M-WEBSITE; MN80M is reading and wondering why he is in the future training girls, these young women training for? Yet he continues to write, so he is viewing all he wrote to them, trying to make sense of it all and his encouragement of them all, they must be good. Lined 1 to 50 messages per day, each day is a lot to handle.

51. Snipers that you are!. Learn until August/September Jets Training for six months from today. One Year Sniper Training!. 6th, maybe 7th, and 8th, each month those days date, plus Jet Training. 27th, 28th, 29th. Each month. Plus any day in between those dates could be training. Any time. Those dates for now. Female from Japan, secure a training day register to sign, you use your own new book, new paper pad of Attendances to training, did they attend or not. Or late. now you know your training room.

THURSDAY,

THURSDAY,

31. A fleet of Lieutenants that be. A fleet of Lieutenants.

32. Just over an hour left to go. Then first day is done for the girls, the young women, The Elite Force Team Greater Russia.

33. A fleet of Lieutenants from the teacher, is great wording. A fleet of Lieutenants is what you are, Sniper Lieutenants that are training to be Jet Pilots. With Sniper being first. A fleet of Snipers, is a fleet of Lieutenants.

34. Training continues Greatly!. Good for the Lieutenants!.

35. "With Sandra," "22 are Perfect!." The teacher will maybe say to me. I would agree with her!. The female from Japan too, I say, and one of the 17+1. The elite force team great Russia. Is near Good enough to be a Colonel, even Lieutenant Colonel, or Assistant Lieutenant Colonel. All Three of Them!. I see how time passes. Thank you!.

36. Sandra, make sure to pay him for three days £81.000, and Still ask the Woman in the accounts department of his payment of £27.000 each day!. Thank you!. Ask her to pay him one payment of £27.000. Then he can send her back £27.000 knowing he got paid. Thank you Sandra!.

37. Everything continues as normal.

38. The females have 25 minutes more of training. I hope well!.

39. The Elite Force Team Greater Russia, after Training, Go to your rooms.

40. The teacher today was brilliant. Only £81.000 for three days, per month. Teaching fee. X 6 months is how much? I can trust him with them!. £486.000 for 6 months, they make me Proud. They are worth it!.

For them to learn Jets Pilot Training, Jets. How to fly one!?. Sandra, after the woman in the accounts department receives the £27.000 back from him, send him X 6 payment of months to come training. £486.000. thank you from me Sandra. Thank you!.

THURSDAY

21. 10 of 17 is good now, so go. Why wait, if for another one of you, you are wasting our time. Time costs learning loss and money!. Do not waste time and wait, just go!.

22. 17+1 get there fastest. To train on how to use a Jet, Jets training, today is the 27th. And tomorrow 28th, and the day after tomorrow the 29th March 2025. Every month 3 days, for three to six months. Go be perfect!. Aggain Success!.

23. Good you won't be late next time at 17 of 21/22 out of the near 24 in The Elite Force Team Greater Russia. The Elite Force Team Great Russia, get there now, it's ok!. Thank you!.

24. Good your all on your way there and some are there already. Good, the female from Japan can sign them in a register if need be, for attendance, of them there, for the record, that gets back to the woman in the accounts

department, from the Teacher to whom he has to let know, so they pay them anything they must.

£6000 each the day of any training for you all The Elite Force Team Greater Russia, with within first The Elite Force Team Great Russia.

Thank you!. 17+1. And ready is female from Ukraine, there, good, Sandra soon if not yet. Sandra go training it's very important from 11:00Hh, to 15:00Hh. Four hours training plus your special, only one allowed to learn and fly the helicopters, maybe a new female if you say we need one for emergency. That is all for now!.

25. Female from Japan, good you are there, plus the female from Ukraine, plus two others, good, tell me more later, enjoy the training. Great teacher to learn from in life Jets training. You are all Russian, don't you forget that!.

26. you are all there learning, good. Good you are learning!.

27. I'm proud of you all!. Keep learning today. Thank you!.

28. Good on until 16:00Hh, 4 oClock. Good full lesson from 11:00Hh to 15:00Hh is because four hours is what it is. So he started by 13:15Hh to 13:35Hh, with all there, then now continue until 16:00 is less time, yet all teaching takes that long to teach today's study.

29. I'm proud of you all. I'm proud!.

30. Learn what to learn for tomorrow. < My Quote, a Quote.

THURSDAY,

THURSDAY,

11. Just get to training fast. Tomorrow is more learning and Saturday, 11:00Hh to 15:00Hh. Thank you!.

12. 17+1+ female from Ukraine, plus female from Thailand plus female from Mexico, all go training, Sandra as well make 21 to 22 with Sandra going to learn Jets.

13. All 21 are Lieutenants.

14. Let me know when you finish. Good!. Just go to training!.

15. The training is a will to learn, even B52 Bombers, and Stealth Mode, perfect training to learn. Over three days of training I told you all last week in writing here, it came Soo quick the day. Go to it, a will to learn flying Jets.

16. Female from Japan, just go without them they will be late, go with the female from Mexico and Thailand. 17 of 17+1, get to the training as quick as possible. For 13:00Hh the latest, learn for two hours and the teacher will bring you up to date. Try never to be late. Thank you for learning. Thank you!. The rest of The Elite Force Team Greater Russia get there quick. Do not sign anything. Just learn.

17. Sandra good work, just get to training. It's important for your helicopter. Learn Jets. Go without them all, or get

17+1+1 to go now quick. If you can, if not just go. Good! Thank you Sandra!.

18. All of The Elite Force Team Greater Russia, make your way to training. Jets training. Sniper Lieutenants.

19. Go there and make me Proud!.

20. Go there and Succeed. The Elite Force Team Greater Russia, you be, and are, Greater Russia.

THURSDAY,

———————————————————————

THURSDAY,

1. The jet training is at 11:00Hh, I do not know the man in training, just go and listen to his teaching of the Jets, the Jets. How they work.

2. Female from Japan, ask him and let him know they are on their way, the Lieutenants, and Sandra must go. It's Jets training.

20 minimum will be there 22 maximum. And tomorrow any more of 24 can be there. Go with 17+1 and tell the girls from Mexico and female from Thailand. Ask the Ukrainian female to go, if she is going. Ask then just go to the Jets training.

3. All The Elite Force Team Greater Russia, training is at 11:00Hh, Jets training, very important. To learn how to fly Jets.

4. Sandra let the teacher know at the end before leaving, the accounts department know it should be £27.000 to him for the three day training, possibly £27.000 each day.

£81.000 total for three days. Thank you, thank him from me, Marshall Law MN80M, Sandra can pay for now.

Sandra if he wants pay him £27.000 each day or £81.000 for the three days, £54.000 is two days. Thank you from me, Thank you!.

5. Sandra we want all three days, 11:00Hh to 15:00Hh. Pay him £81.000 for three days or we can let the accounts department to pay him when they do. Ask him, and tell once you finish training the woman in the accounts department. Thank you Sandra, Good Morning!. For 22 that are ready to train, 22 new Lieutenants, to learn how to fly Jets.

6. Female from Japan, just get them ready to go to the training, and tell them where it is. Go with them together with some of them or most of them. 17+1 +1 go to training for 11:00am/Hh to 3:00pm/15:00Hh.

Four hours of jet training. Good! And tomorrow and the day after the same learning of how to fly a jet, the lecturer / teacher is good, he will explain and teach how, they are powerful Jets. Especially the ones I bought for you all to use. Learn from a teacher. 11:00am/11:00Hh.

7. Female from Japan, once they know go with them or on own is ok. Try go together now and not be late. Girls get up and go fast. Young women, Lieutenants, wake up, wash face quickly and go. Female from Japan you get there first then with any other going. Just go. It's ok. You told them, thank you!. Sandra it's £6000 each to those that go the training payment. For you and the other young women that go. Each day, thank you!. £18.000 for the three days training. Thank you!

8. Go to the Training!. The youngest can go!. Thank you!.

9. 17+ 1, Get to the training. Female from Ukraine get to the Training. Good to go!.

10. Female from Japan, just go on your own then, leave them be late, not you!. Tell the teacher one of them is delaying the others as she wants to rest and do it tomorrow and has been told no. She must go today first day of training on Jets.

THURSDAY,

WEDNESDAY,

21. The Elite Force Team Greater Russia, Yes, they can have those pistols I own. Thank you! The new ones each in the boxes room. The female from Thailand and the female from Mexico. Thank you! Thank you!

22. Thank you to the "Elite Force Team Greater Russia", for all they do. Thank you!. For all you do!. Thank you!.

23. Female from Japan, it's ok, take the sniper rifle back to your room and put it in the closet, you are being perfect, thank you, get some rest, your own personal ones are all success, a blis, blissful. Thank you!.

24. I'm tired, I'm going to sleep soon. Thank you!.

25. Female from Ukraine I hope you are ok and well. Keep wearing your pistols, your perfect. Put them in your closet for two days if you like. Thank you from me, thank you!.

26. 17+1 keep them on you until night then take them off 17 at about 22:00Hh to 23:00Hh start times to take it off and keep them safely in your closet.

27. Thank you to all, Thank you!.

28. Nothing more was written here!.

29. Nothing more was written here!.

30. Nothing more was written here!.

WEDNESDAY,

WEDNESDAY,

11. The female from Japan. Make sure they understand.

12. Model them, then take a 19 minutes to show off boldly your responsibility, of holding a gun. To hip. To back. To waist, like me, is perfection and not just difficult, serious and difficult for most to do, Model them. At female from Mexico and female from Thailand. Then one hour 18 minutes after the hour pass, as you passing by as many as you know and new in life, belt, and Seatbelt, and Waist Belt. Good!.wear strong.

13. Good for you both at female from Thailand and Mexico.

14. 14 is too young to be in military, tell him, her, to go back home soon and stay with mum and go to school. Not Military. Who is responsible for the 14 year old? Is she one of 17+1, female from Japan Find Out.

15. Sandra pay her £30.000. the youngest of the team The Elite Force Team Great Russia. The Elite Force Team Greater Russia.

16. 17+1 vallahii, belirng, cocuk is young, should be at home with mum.

17. 17+1.The should get off in Colombia, and fly home to Cyprus, or Turkey, be safe with mum. She should get off safely.

18. Sandra if one is 16, give her the same, £30.000, then, the one younger or first. Give them both £30.000 each. Thank you Sandra, Thank you, Thank you!.

19. 17+1 make sure your money is in order. And that they are safe. The next stop, is Colombia, they both get off safely, and one other 17 year old female equals £90.000. Sandra should pay £60.000 to £90.000. 17+1 tell her the amount. Two or Three like that!. Very young!.

20. Thank you for saying you will let me know.

WEDNESDAY,

WEDNESDAY,

1. Good Morning!.

2. Thailand Female, and Mexican Female, Read all the Sniper Positions, see my diagrams, learn position, most easiest up. Then read her, then read Sniper Range. Then here for a post for you to read Lieutenants.

3. Druyzna, get 80 more of the diamonds get 80 more Purple Ones. Small medium size for £50 million or £10 million. Purple Ones. For the elite force team greater Russia. And to have on you to my choice. Thank you!

4. Female from Japan, can you ask the girl from the boxes room to be ready and prepared to give the female from Thailand and Mexico, their foxes, two of them. The black one or the silver one for them first, to have that I own, as I own the ship, and everything new on board delivered for my say of how to use. To be ready with what she gave you all, The Elite Force Team Great Russia. And one Ukraine

female only if she not have hers yet. She should. She is in The Elite Force Team Greater Russia. Thank you! 19:00 is Good!.

5. 348, then 1000 young women will be receiving Foxes. They must only use when I tell them to use it, and when I tell one of you The Elite Force Team Greater Russia to tell them to use it, to use one or both or any. That is a rule. To defend the ship. To defend intelligence.

6. If the females use it without permission they are to be removed off of ship. They are not to be used personally.

7. The Elite Force Team Greater Russia how are you all doing ok? How is your day?

8. Female from Turkish 17, do a follow up on the Jets training in a room on the 27th with the Japanese female. 27th, 28th, 29th the without e. Of March 2025, if only one day then Good Thank you!. 17+1. The Elite Force Team Great Russia the elite force team greater Russia. All 21 of 24, Sandra is not on ship Rebecca is. Rebecca is. I hope you are all doing good and are ok.

9. Female from Japan, the female from Thailand and Mexico are to receive their Foxes Tonight, make sure they know how to wear them, when they receive them at 08:47pm / 20:47Hh. They are both good for one they are Lieutenants. Both Russian, one from Mexico and One From Thailand.

10. Female from Thailand be safe with them both, wear them both first, then at night just the black one after 21:00Hh. For you and the female from Mexico 22:00. For both safety of ship. And you all. Not for personal use, try this for few days. Do as the Japanese female tells you to wear it which times, then go with it, and how she shows you it should be in your bag in your locker. Thank you from me. Thank you!

WEDNESDAY,

TUESDAY,

11. Three more days until the female from Ukraine gets her own Sniper Rifle, or four or five more days?

12. One more day until tomorrow until the females from Thailand and Mexico get their Gun / Pistol, both of them, the Silver and Black one.

13. Female from Japan Ohayoo Gozaimasu! O Genki Desu Ka? Is all good with you? How is Everything? With you!? Good female from Japan. Good Morning!. Tomorrow afternoon, the two young women can get their Foxes. Tell them tonight how to wear it. Thank you! You rest!. I hop

14. Female from Ukraine continue as normal, this life way is a good normal. What you did was correct, to show them like that how to use the Sniper Rifle, my trust to you on that is correct. Thank you! Be Good today, have a simple day, relax some more your body needs it. Thank you. 5 more days until you get your brand new Sniper Rifle, be Good

with it. Silencer might be good too. You will see once you get one. Thank you!

15. The Elite Force Team Greater Russia, training yesterday was serious, and how it should be. Some Jokes and Laughter for the day should be with it all. To allow you all to be serious with a sense of humor. Like laughter when the girls all became a Lieutenant.

The day is nothing to do today. Be around for the team, get some fresh air alone. The Elite Force Team Great Russia, be normal, how are your Foxes? Wear them good, daily. Tell me how you feel with them all on you.

The Elite Force Team Greater Russia, Tell me how you feel as well. Today see what they see, not much to do. Always something to do. On board and off board. Be calm and relaxed day, be wiser, you are all Lieutenants to the two new.

Two new can have like Sandra, a number here with me, every number pertains to them, or numbers they are, you are, 23 or 24, each numbered here daily, next is 16, no numbers 23, and 24 just to you.

Personal numbers of this contact with you to read to coach you through this you train for and now anything to do with this all and Sniper Training.

Some things personal for yourself, other things for them, most for the team, teams, The Elite Force Team Great Russia and The Elite Force Team Greater Russia.

You are The Elite Force Team Greater Russia. 22/24 supposed to be in Total. 24 people.

17+1 +1 +2. + Sandra/Rebecc, equals 22. She gets number 19 here. And more with all in general. Sometimes three posts to four blog posts to several people before like The Elite Force Team Great Russia female from Japan in The Elite Force Team Greater Russia with you both, I hope the easiness not be seen weak, it's difficult to do this all.

They just make it look easy they are Soo good. The female from Ukraine was nervous yesterday, she had to do her job. Do exactly as I say, and write, and find yourself greatness in you to be seen and known. Thank you for Sniper Training and each day that passes, you could yes get asked to help, there is payments for that all. Earn greater Health.

I hope you care, as those that do, do as they do. The Elite Force Team Greater Russia. Being Greater!

16. No one has 16 yet!?!.

17. 17+1 I just heard some. Good you went at that time in the morning. Plus at the end to clear apples some of you all. Thank you! Be ready for your Snipers from today. Wear them, get them from tomorrow, be prepared for one like her one, and after it's on the bed you girls, young women, put them safe as she can show you in your closets, the female from Japan.

Thank you all, each day for what you do, and success you accomplish on your own, thank you. From me, Marshal Law MN80M.

The Owner. Age 14 a Green Beret, age 41 White Beret. With a purple blue heart with embroidery around it. Green Beret White Beret, with that in-between. ("Cromanant") In-between.

45 years old, weeks ago, last month, and still the same. I am. Like you would all be green berets. Starting new passed some military tests to get into the military. Then some to army, some remain in military work all their life.

18. The Elite Force Team Greater Russia be ready after you all have your Rifles, Sniper Rifles, the elite force team some 438 could be, all rest on ship, get a gun or two each.

Two each, they must not use it for anything else that is not to be used for in life. And most to keep it in their closet after the first week. No need to carry them both everyday. Monday,Tuesday, Wednesday Yes, off Thursday, Friday, Saturday is Greatest for them all to do, and Sunday.

The Elite Force Team Greater Russia you must wear yours everyday holding one on you in the ways you do. Seatbelt and Belt. Good, ok. You got one week before them all and you have the Sniper Rifle. Be great with them on you. Female from Japan, yes you can wear your one now to go out to them all. Good! Thank you for asking!.

19. Sandra how is your day? Are you and Rebecca ok? Did she say anything about the team?, is she in or not!?. Thank you! You say, Sometimes the people are like animal." Treatment them like one then, ignore them and don't talk to animals. Be away from negatives.

Tell me more when you can, Alexin wants to come back on board with my permission, I say Yes! Let me know what you can be done to make the place better for him, same room and more space for him? If possible, the Vodka he can bring lots of for prizes, 1000 bottle with him, and rare Vodka's, I agree to him doing, it's ok. How about with you all that met him? Some military stripes or Medals, like Diamonds has a best Friend, He is the Owner of every country and the Sotheby's around the World. True.!.

Gold medals I want him to get some or I can just buy them and through things I own, Like Sotheby's and Fort Knox, ask him when you see him next.

20. Sandra, paying them all is greatness to, a lot of you.

TUESDAY,

TUESDAY,

1. Good morning! Minimal posts today.

2 Usual day!. Thank you!.

3. I'm resting for today. Thank you!.

4. At the elite force team, be normal. Lieutenants!

5. At 17+1, thank you for not letting me wait, The Elite Force Team great Russia yesterday. 06:47Hh, you were with the female from Japan. Perfect!. Female from Japan perfect arranging arrangements. Where to go and what to do at what time, you should all tell me and not just two or three. Good you all did that mission, even the ones that could have gone, thank you. See she came to my door, her door the female from Japan, and is not a time waster. True!.

6. Go to the bathroom time waster time. And not waste time. Confirm I heard everything you were saying. I will back to you.

7. Light duties for today. Good for some, to do. Relax some.

8. Female from Japan , Did other girls, young women in the elite force team great Russia, dispose of the apples into the sea. Who did? At the end when it finished.

Who did the clean up, picking up and throwing into the sea as I said they could be? Even picking up and putting it into a box then in to the sea.

I hope one of The Elite Force Team Great Russia. I asked in written here for them to go and the others to go back down to room, to help the female from Japan that way. Good the ones that did, that's £3000 each for helping out on that day, yesterday.

The other three Lieutenants, that's £9000 each, for doing that mission, The Elite Force Team Greater Russia. The Elite Force Team Great Russia. Good! Sandra should pay them and confirm to me their pay. Good for you all.

9. Beauty is completing training!.

10. Female from Japan, Last night, I heard the time she came to you, not all the rest. Try few words to save long good speech. What then next, ? What time? Then next? What happened!?. How comes many hours passed before upstairs with after the apples. And I heard in the past half an hour.

TUESDAY,

MONDAY,

31. Being there cares.

32. Always be with each other, even when 3hours apart to 8hours apart, Lieutenants. Always be with each other!.

33. Female from Japan when you can, Go and see them personal, old teams and people you know and knew on ship, and life so far with Sniper Training. See some old friends, have your foxes with you only.

34. Female from Thailand and Mexico female, I hope you got paid!. Congratulations on completing training, you are both now Lieutenants. Wake up strong!.

35. Be free, be wise.

36. The Elite Force Team Great Russia, how are all 17 + 1? All of you Pink students, students of Pink in Turkish is what? We/I hope that you are all ok!. That's good Pembe's students of English Language when young, I checked into you all. Those if from there knowing Lefkosa, Ekdovan, Yegitler first. Lefke. Not Pembe's Lefkosa, Cyprus my family also from, The Turkish side, your Good. Keep going strongly. By them and I. How are you all. Be normal. How you finding using the foxes on you. Does it look good on you, and on you all?

37. (Nothing here to write, the day ended)

38. (Nothing here to write, the day ended)

39. (Nothing here to write, the day ended)

40. (Nothing here to write, the day ended)

MONDAY,

21. Greatly going, and then Gone! The Elite Force Team Greater Russia is the best thing ever.

22. Congratulations to all The Elite Force Team Greater Russia, two new more than one, Two new Lieutenants. Russian Thailand, one, another Mexican Russian. Both Russian. Both real life Lieutenants. They will be great lieutenant's and greatly appreciated as a Sniper.

23. Congratulations to the one from Thailand and one from Mexico that respected and listened to the female from Japan and did as she said. And good for the female from Thailand, to trust her as well. Both Lieutenants!

24. Good for you Women!!!!.

25. The Russian Military Ship, I own, as Marshal Law, and Owner of everything I own, and more.

26. A military ship, has 17 Turkish females, 1 Japanese female, 1 Ukraine Ukrainian, 1 from Thailand Russian, and 1 Mexican, from Mexico. All Russian!. Plus Sandra + Rebecca. All Lieutenants! All perfect! Mission Accomplished. 21 Lieutenants, now I Train 21 Lieutenants to 23/24. With Sandra and Rebecca. Two positions, leave 21 any time for the female in the boxes room. And 22 for the Ukrainian. They might change mind or attitude as the Ukraine one new did, then she's trying to be a boss. She is not the team. The team made themselves go to train, they earned being a Lieutenant. The earned to be a Lieutenant. 17+1+1. For sure The elite force team great Russia the elite force team greater Russia. 21 Snipers. Two have 15 tasks before they do become one officially, Soo simple they will finish that. Wash hands and face.

27. A military ship, has 17 Turkish females, 1 Japanese female, 1 Ukraine Ukrainian, 1 from Thailand Russian, and 1 Mexican, from Mexico. All Russian!. Plus Sandra + Rebecca. All Lieutenants! All perfect! = 21 fully trained

by Owner, all sophisticated!. All to be Legends, someday. Greatly at Sniper Rifle!

These women remain serious! I hope they become Adult and wise, just keep it on you, don't go to anyone's once you have it.

Be Good, with it, yet weary if any fear from it. Truth to your safety. Thank you! Thank you! 23 + 24 = 47, stick together with them, 17+1, plus training girl, the female from Ukraine in training room.

She is very Good, what happened was she was being bullied into doing things wrong for me and us all. So we removed the threat, I did for her. No more other girl for this, not even talk until now. I hope her attitude has changed, her mentality. This other girl I mean. Anyway, you all did good. Thank the female from Japan when you can.

28. Sandra how are you? Tell me your day! Have you been ok? How is your sister!?. I hope you are both ok!.

29. Female from Japan, keep telling me your day. How was the start, what time? Then after? Then any contact from me here or any was from what time? Thank you from me, Thank you!. You are appreciated!.

Keep it safe in your closet. Next to your bed, and relax some, use the foxes to wear, belt and seatbelt. And walk around some different!. Feel more alert and bold sophisticated walk. Wearing your foxes, like checking up on work!. Thank you!.

65

30. Rebecca, Sandra, which one I choose to always talk to? Rebecca. Could not handle being serious and most loyal. Sandra, did you pay them all yet Rebecc. Sandra and or you, which one for payments, Rebecca. Good, girls if you need money right now let Rebecca know quick. Let Rebecca know. Sandra/Rebecca, pay them all. Good day I hope! Why start negative, O them, well, stay away from them negative talk negative people.

MONDAY,

MONDAY,

11. You are all doing very good!

12. Keep going until the end! All 11 positions, how many Apples they shot each? Tell me all once you are all back to your rooms safely. To Lieutenants that exist to Lieutenants that are existing. Finish Greatly, go back to rooms once done.

13. Two females in training when you read this I say, "Good training!." To the females from Thailand and Mexico, Good Training. Once you wake tomorrow, you are a Lieutenant, as you completed the training from morning until now 13:12Hh.

Well done, brilliant work done, finish off any last things apart from shooting the apples you both can ask. Then back to your rooms.

Finish training, even something with team, at night, to do, if able four more days until a pistol/ gun. Maybe a week!. Maybe tonight!

Don't worry about it!. I hope and we're glad we did training as it's supposed to go. Thank you! Thank you from me, Thank you!.

Maybe being Lieutenants by night is same, do less you still become a Lieutenant. The Elite Force Team Greater Russia.

14. Sandra £6000, each for training until now 13:19Hh / 13:22Hh time. £27.000 to the female from Ukraine helping me to train them Sniper Rifle Training. The Elite Force Team Greater Russia. The others their amounts. 4 x 9000 +1 £16000. Female from Japan £16.000 plus £9000. Three Turkish Girls £9000 each, two more equals five of them £3000 each. £3000 to the ones after cleaning up the apples, throw the apples off deck.

15. Two new Lieutenants are Lieutenants. When they wake they will be lieutenant's.

16. All others, keep going on finish. Then back to room

17. Female from Japan let me know how you do. How you are doing? Tell me everything of your day.

18. All others continue in what you are in, a blessing. Finish!.

19. Sandra, pay them £9000 each, The female from Thailand and the female from Mexico. And £27.000 to the female from Ukraine.19 is you.

20. The day is Good!. 18:33 'We finished the day". Greatly said by female from Japan.

MONDAY,

_____

MONDAY,

1. Keep it in your locker safe. Walk around with foxes only few hours or more than wear one fox only. Sandra has tried to stop things, but she must make payment, she accepted the 5 million and said no more she can do once it's finished. For her maybe, for you all, your safe. Military!.

2. Keep the sniper rifle safe in your room.

3. Good training tell her to remember the O. The girl female from Thailand and Mexico, to remember their written training.

4. Female from Japan, make sure she knows. The training written will help her target better. No answers about training unless your in The Elite Force Team Greater Russia.

Keep going 5 minutes per position, 10 bullets each time. To Position 11. The "O" the target is an apple this time. Complete missions greatly Lieutenant. So far, Good Job.

Great working so far, tell the 17+1 they can go back down anytime good job done mission.

Stay with them now and complete. Then to room for everyone, let me know when you are, in room. Mission accomplished!. When they finished, and go to their room, ask two more females from 17+1 The Elite Force Team Great Russia, to help you clean up the apples. £3000 each they will get, and then to their room.

Good so far different with Coaching!. Thank you!. £9000 to each three one other maybe helped get the apples, = 3 were with you female from Japan, making is 4 x £9000. Should at first be £3000 you succeeded and did more great things to success, focus on those two girls now with female from Ukraine. £9000 each to four of you. Mission Accomplished. Lieutenants.

Keep going with training. Let the female from Ukraine say what she told you all, must be the same or not much of she not advising them on what to do. She must finish it with them passing is Success. £27.000 to her today. She must finish work though. Good girl, young lady, young woman. Once she is finished, clear up the apples. No talk of anyone else's wanna be training.

5. 17+1 mission accomplished. Go to your rooms, tell them to "remember the Manuel, the training." To the two new females tell the females that before leaving.

6. Female from Thailand "remember the "O".

7. Female from Mexico, good shooting and learning fast. Remember the "O" and good holding the breath.

8. The female from Ukraine can take a break. 15 minutes to use the bathroom and break down stairs, then complete training. Thank you! Thank you!.

9. The female from Mexico is doing ok, goooooood!. The female from Thailand is goood ok Good!.

10. The female from Ukraine is doing very good!. Very well. Continue on, and then to your room. For an hour before you leave the room for any reason an hour later or to get some fresh air.

From the room, good updating at break, £27.000 for your day working helping me to train them, you, female from Ukraine.

Thank you, your nearly done training, until next month sniper rifle training. More about the rifle. Very good, Brilliant work in the room. In the training room, I await an update on all, later, finish work, finish training for today Lieutenant number 19. There is always work to do!

MONDAY,

SUNDAY,

31. Success is what you have attained!

32. Female girl from Japan. Wear your belt with fox on it, then your shoulder strap a other fox in it, plus your sniper rifle in hands and shoulder strap. Colt 18 Sniper Rifle, and your number is 18, 18th into The Elite Force Team Great Russia. Wear them all and go around point finger the right way. You are Trusted with me. Thank you! Thank you! Thank you!. For being you, thank you!

33. When you finish letting all docks know, go to the Straight Tower, the Tower men, let them see you holding foxes and the Sniper Rifle in hand, then Salut to him for me. Female from Japan.

34. Sandra the second you have their bank number do it. Pay the female from Thailand and the female from Mexico £6000 each, one or both The female from Japan can get them to sign for me. You pay them and £4000 more, plus £2000 from yesterday = 10.000/12.000 each one. Thank you!.give them £12.000 payment. Sandra pay them 12000 each. Thank you!

35. Female from Japan continue on perfect, few seconds use finger as taught on metal. To perfection. An unknown way of doing things with a new alien way of life. To perfection, no talking, in English and Japanese.

36. Remember to keep it going. Never stay in same place for more than seconds, walk from far they see be stronger than any of thee.

37.Let me know when it's Poetry week.

38. Female from Japan give me an Update from last night until now, how is things with you? Eating good, resting good? Feeling? With work? Then all!.

39.Wear it on your right hand side of hip, like John Wayne. ready.

40. Female from Japan go around with the foxes on you, plus that, you were to them, them looking for them just to say Hi to them all, The Elite Force Team Greater Russia. Then go back to your room. Just go around in silence like one sweep. Of Air.

SUNDAY,

---

21. Do not do anything on your own and never for any one else.

22. 13:00Hh has just passed 13 Hundred hours. Why are they not finished? Tell me!. They can go back to their rooms.

23. The female from Ukraine was paid £288.000 to train the elite force team greater Russia all year, not money for anything else, that's a job she has to do, not anyone else, it's simple, even the girl from Japan can do it.

24. Female from 17+1, The Elite Force Team Great Russia, Turkish Origin, you that choice to, will you go two of you for this and the Japanese female. A team mission, do you agree.!?.?! If so, and Yes, then simple!. Wake up and go by 07:15amHh. To get the apples.

To get the Apples, and go up on top deck, lay them down in 10/20 layer straight position, each 10 / 20 row of Apples. Lay out 50. Go with the female from Japan this mission. When ended, go to training room in the morning early this shall be 15/20 minutes of laying them down on the ground the three of you placing. Go into the training room and observe and watch them go up with the female from Ukraine to the shooting range the Sniper Range where you three laid down the apples for their training to complete. Then, go back to your room and leave them to finish, complete this mission perfect.

Be in the training room by 07:30Hh. Thank you for tomorrow!.

25. Female from Ukraine, be in the training room before 07:00amHh. Complete training with them all by 08:30 / 09:00 then keep telling me training is over. Thank you! You can let some know who are in touch with me how things are going with you from morning. Thank you!

Tomorrow morning, 07:00Hh, train them after they read the Manuel contract, and await three or two of The Elite Force Team Great Russia there to help you The Elite Force Team Greater Russia with them you are greater.

You will go upstairs with the two new trainees that by tomorrow, will finish greatly and become the final two Lieutenants for months. Maybe a year and longer. So go with them up, then as you did with all the girls young women, tell them what you say, then complete positions 1 to 11. Aim, Shot, Fire. Launch fire. Pull trigger. Aim fire.

Be aware, they all love you, others don't.

The Elite Force Team Greater Russia. On your own from others, you are greater. Just get up and go once they come down into the training room. I hope you are ok, try to complete four on your own after the young women do, one from Mexico Russian, One from Thailand Russian. Bot Russians.

Work well Russian Lieutenant Blonde Ukrainian Blond hair. Most blonde. Any colour is good on you. Be wise, be respectful, new Lieutenants to be, your newly one too. I hope you rest for today after it all, only first thing in the morning. Tomorrow the same.

26. Good work today Lieutenant's!

27. A female from Japan, you have a mission tomorrow, Do you accept? The Mission is simple, yet be safe from the sea. What to do if you ask?

To get the Apples, and go up on top deck, lay them down in 10/20 layer straight position, each 10 / 20 row of Apples. Lay out 50. Go with two females in 17+1 you The Elite Force Team Great Russia on this mission.

When ended, go to training room in the morning early this shall be 15/20 minutes of laying them down on the ground the three of you placing. Go into the training room and observe and watch them go up with the female from Ukraine to the shooting range the Sniper Range where you three laid down the apples for their training to complete. Then, go back to your room and leave them to finish, complete this mission perfect.

You can stay on as an observer, the three of you or one of them only if they want and choice. Thank you! By 07:00Hh, be up there start laying apples, 07:05Hh Start 06:47Hh, get early and finish quick early. You make me proud of you!.

I'm sure those two as well also become greater, and knows the same from me, some day. Thank you! For no shouting and arguments. No trouble. Thank you!.

At girl in team 17+1 the Elite Force Team Great Russia. Their superior, happy birthday to whichever one of those it is, Turkish females from Turkey or Cyprus Russian. Happy birthday Recent and to come any birthday.

Payment is £3000 each, could be Payment is £3000+£16000=19000 for this mission I would give. Payment is £3000 only this time from me again. (3000/16000/9000) 28000 in total each. £9000 total Rebecca could pay can pay them each £3000 x 3, you and the two females = £9000. Mission no price to me the Owner. You should do it with her in the morning, she will inspire you the female from Japan will inspire you. Do the mission, be One of 'two of you', to go with her. The female from Japan.

28. The female from Ukraine, you will get £27.000 for today, but for doing what you must on two more positions open, 21+22 is no one yet. So it's only 20 women, twenty young Women. Then, The female from Mexico, 23 then the female from Thailand 24. The elite force team Greater Russia. Go get some rest female from Ukraine.

29. Sandra, pay her £28.000 for Today. The female from Ukraine.

The females continued through their day. MN80M-THE-SPECIAL-ONE-MALE is wondering what in the future he is doing by wasting time, training them, when no training is better to everyone. Less heartache when some not get trained. MN80M reads upwards now, from this page back to chapter 10 "Our Lives" of the same view he saw. Then stops to read the ending here. Monday,

1. All those in training is good!. All those to get to training do now. Thank you! Unless unwell, if unwell stay in bed or if you need to rest.

2. All those in training is good!.

3. Female from Ukraine, Very Good! Extremely Good!.

4. Female from Japan, Very Good! Definitely Good!.

5. 7 have hit 7, and with their own Rifles. Sniper Rifle!.

6. Success is going to training. Success is completing training. Success is both!.

7. Remember the training, my training. Continue Brilliantly!.

8. Female from Japan, When, hitting 8 apples with bullets from their own Sniper Rifle feels Good, 100% Lawful, they can then go back to their rooms. Tomorrow do it all until 11. Thank you!. Any Rifle, Incase the female from Ukraine uses a different One.

9. Female from Japan, let them continue until 8 apples they hit, then go back to rooms, Great Training Good Job, Well done!. 8 today and 8 tomorrow.

10. Female from Japan, Finish Brilliantly like that written above, until 8 apples each has been hit. Finish From position 8.

In 33 target hit, how many is done? There has been a minimum 8 to 12. Good very good it is. In 33 target hit, how many is done? Minimum 8 to 12. Good very good it is. See Russian girls, are young Women. Russian Snipers. Trained on an Intelligence Ship, by Marshal Law MN80M. The Owner.

Female from Japan, you go try it first from position 8 on my drawings, in the Sniper Range and other blogs with title Sniper, look for some of my drawings there for training. Position eight is right side next to the middle, just nearer to the end of side of ship. Just walk out and walk 14 steps from middle right side outwards.

Is position eight like 11 is then further up Ship, behind the middle part when going up top deck turn left position 11 and 10, turn right, position 9, 8, 7, 6, 5, 4, and position 3. Position 1, 2, in the other part. Position One is and position two, the other side of top deck the ship. Try to memorize that, and know your positions to perfection, on the Snipers Range, Top Deck.

With your own Guns, Sniper Rifle, you hit more than one target.

With your own Guns, Sniper Rifle, you hit the target. Sniper Rifle Success, it does Work Brilliantly. See, much better to have waited for the Sniper Rifle. I'm proud of you all.

Tomorrow, some more same training. Thank you! Thank you for training from me, Thank you!. Female from Japan, throw those hit rotten apples and others cotton, throw them all off ship. Ask the Eldest Turkish female from them all, to Help you with two others now quickly. The training is near complete, once back in room.

Ask the female from Ukraine to help you as well, to throw those apples from ship to sea. Thank you from me!.

The female from Ukraine can practice on top deck more tomorrow from 11:00 to 12:00, on her Own. Starting position One. To 11, position 1 to 11. Or position: 1,2,11,10,9,8,7,6,5,4,3. Try that tomorrow morning female from Ukraine. The female from Japan, 1, 2, 3, 4, 5, 6, 7, 8, 9, 10, and position 11, is Final. 8 is Brilliant, Superb Brilliant is you, the female from Japan. You are all being Brilliant, this is very good for you all. Female from Japan, and if you want to take one more shot you can from position 3 or position 1.

Your choice. Position 9 is Good!. Go for it!. Success!. I'm with you!. All others continue on!

Flashback------------------------------

17:15 2023 MN80M is in LONDON, ENGLAND, UNITED KINGDOM. IN CONTACT COMMUNICATION WITH THE DON OF ITALY, JOHN GOTTI.

MN80M
John Gotti, you are the Don of Italy as I the Owner of both including Sicilly. You are always the Don to me. Don Gotti, of Italy, American.

DON JOHN GOTTI
Think he be me, they think, as if I not want my reign. I am John Gotti of Italy. Don CC, of Sicily.

MN80M
You are Don Gotti to me.

JOHN GOTTI
Thank you, from me!

MN80M is in LONDON, ENGLAND, UNITED KINGDOM. IN CONTACT COMMUNICATION

WITH THE DON OF ITALY, JOHN GOTTI. Then comes to a halt.

Flashback--------------------

2011 CAIRO, EGYPT, TAHRIR SQUARE.

o   MN80M is alone in the Square.

---Flashback----------------------

2011 CAIRO, EGYPT, TAHRIR SQUARE . "The time is now, I am here." "Im here I said." MN8OM THE-SPECIAL-ONE-MALE looks at his MN8OM- SQUARE-WATCH again. Then up to the sky, at the Eagle flying by that then turns in formation movement down some towards MN8OM. "Im here". He said, and then moves faster than normal back into the centre of the square, Tahrir Square, Cairo, Egypt. "I'm here" he said while walking forward the same with her, MN80M-THE-SPECIAL-ONE-FEMALE.

The End!

Printed in the United States
by Baker & Taylor Publisher Services